W9-BSQ-372

Braceville Elementary School
District # 75
Braceville, Ill. 60407

By Muriel Stanek

NEW IN THE CITY
ONE, TWO, THREE FOR FUN
LEFT, RIGHT, LEFT, RIGHT!
TALL TINA

I Won't Go Without a Father

Muriel Stanek
Illustrated by Eleanor Mill

ALBERT WHITMAN & COMPANY, CHICAGO

ISBN 0-8075-3524-9; Library of Congress Card Number 78-188435

Published simultaneously in Canada by George J. McLeod, Limited, Toronto
Lithographed in the United States of America.

A Note About This Story

Many children come from one-parent homes. The reason may be death, desertion, or divorce, and each of these children must eventually come to terms with this situation. Steve, whose story is told here, has moments of jealousy and loneliness when he sees someone else with a father. He feels cheated and thinks that he is the only one with this problem.

Planning for a school event to which parents are invited brings Steve's problem to a crisis. He slowly comes to realize that he is not the only child without both parents. Warm and affectionate relatives and friends help him find sources of adult companionship and counsel, and this makes the situation more acceptable even if it cannot alter the circumstances.

This story may open the way for some children of one-parent homes to face their own feelings as they identify with Steve. When feelings and thoughts are shared, the problem is often seen in a more realistic perspective than when it is repressed. Understanding grows that happy family relationships may encompass the greater family circle and extend to grandparents, uncles, aunts, cousins, and even friends and neighbors.

MURIEL STANEK

OPEN HOU
NEXT
WEDN

Steve didn't have a father. He never talked about it. But sometimes he felt a little sad or a little jealous when he saw other boys with their dads.

One day at school, Steve's teacher said, "Open House will be next Wednesday evening. Your mothers and fathers are invited to come and see your work."

Planning for the special school program began right away. Everyone felt excited.

At first Steve was excited, too. Then he remembered he'd be coming alone with his mother.

He thought, "Everybody at school will see that I don't have a father. I won't go. I'm going to stay home."

He had his mind made up, and that was that.

At home, Steve did not tell his mother about the Open House.

"If she doesn't know, she can't do anything about it," he told himself. "And if I don't go, I won't have to watch old Ronnie's father acting important."

It was getting dark. Steve looked out the window. The streetlights were just going on. People were coming home from work.

Steve saw Ronnie running to meet his father at the bus stop. Ronnie's father had a big smile the way he always did. He handed Ronnie a box to carry home. He always did that, too.

Steve looked away. He thought to himself, "That Ronnie thinks he's something special."

Then Steve began to worry. How could he keep his mother from knowing about the Open House at school on Wednesday night? He pulled the shade down and walked into the kitchen. His mother was making supper.

"What did my dad really look like?" he asked his mother for the hundredth time.

"He looked quite a lot like you," answered Mrs. Blakeman. "Is there any special reason why you are asking?"

Steve shook his head.

He took a small picture of his father from his pocket and looked at it for a long time.

"I wish I could remember him," he said.

Just then the doorbell at the back rang. It was Jennifer from next door.

"Let me in!" she called. "I have something for you."

Steve put the picture in his pocket before he opened the door.

"Hello, Mrs. Blakeman! Hello, Steve!" Jennifer exclaimed. "My mother made cupcakes today. Here are some for you."

"Thank you," said Mrs. Blakeman.

"Are you and Steve going to the Open House at school next Wednesday?" asked Jennifer. "All the mothers and fathers are invited to come to school to see our work."

Mrs. Blakeman glanced at Steve in surprise. He hadn't said a thing about the meeting.

"I forgot to tell you about it," Steve said quickly. "Besides, I don't want to go to that old meeting."

He ran into his bedroom and slammed the door. "Big mouth, Jennifer," he muttered. "I wish she'd go home."

After Jennifer left, Mrs. Blakeman went into Steve's room. He was looking cross.

"What's the matter?" asked his mother.

"Nothing," answered Steve.

"Then tell me about the Open House at school."

"I don't want to go!" Steve said. "I'll be the only kid without a father."

"That isn't so," said Mrs. Blakeman. "Besides, there's nothing to be ashamed of in not having a father. Come, let's eat our supper now."

That evening, Steve and his mother hardly spoke a word.

"Steve, honey," his mother said at last. "Lots of children don't have both parents. It's too bad. But that's the way it is. They must learn to get along with the family and friends they have."

"Who needs a father anyway?" Steve asked himself. He sat in the big chair and stared at the lamp on the table.

His eyes were half closed so that the light seemed blurred. Steve pretended to see his father's face in the light.

The next morning as Steve was getting ready for school, Mrs. Blakeman said, "Shall I call Uncle John at the army camp? Maybe he can get off long enough to come with us to the school meeting Wednesday night."

Steve shrugged his shoulders. He liked his Uncle John, but it wasn't the same as having a father.

His mother said, "Go to Grandpa's house after school, Steve. This is one of my late days at work."

At school, the children talked about the Open House.

"Our best papers and drawings will be around the room for our parents to see," Karen said. "I can hardly wait for my mother and dad to see all the work I've done."

"She makes me sick," said Steve under his breath. "I hate girls."

Steve walked over to a group of boys.

"Are your parents coming to the Open House?" asked Ronnie.

""I don't know," answered Steve. "Who cares about the dumb old meeting?"

"My father works nights," Tom said, "and my mother is sick. Do you think my big sister can come in their place?"

"Sure," said Billy. "Guess what! I'm going to have two mothers and two fathers come to the Open House."

"You're making that up," said Steve.

"No, I'm not," Bill said. "My real mother and father are divorced. They each got married again. Now I have two mothers and two fathers."

"Well, that's better than not having any father," said Steve.

But Billy said, "That's what you think."

After school, Steve went to Grandpa's house.

"Your mother called and asked me to trim your hair," Grandpa said. "Hop into the chair."

"Do I have to get it cut?" asked Steve.

"Yes," answered Grandpa. "We won't be able to see your face if it gets much longer."

Steve climbed up on a high stool. Grandpa tied a big towel around Steve's neck and began to trim his hair.

"What's ailing you, son?" asked Grandpa. "You look as if you lost your last friend."

"I don't want to go to the Open House at school on Wednesday night," Steve explained.

"Why not?" asked Grandpa.

"It's for mothers and fathers. Who wants to go with only his mother?"

"How does your mother feel about all this?" wondered Grandpa.

"I don't know."

"What do you think your father would want you to do?"

Steve shrugged his shoulders.

As he walked home, Steve thought about what Grandpa had said. His mother's feelings might be hurt, but he still didn't want to go to the Open House.

"If only I had a big brother," Steve thought. "He'd help me. But what's the use of wishing?"

When Steve got near home, he saw his mother and Mr. Green, their neighbor. Steve felt sure they were talking about him.

"How would you like to come and help me work on my old car Saturday, Steve?" asked Mr. Green.

When Steve nodded, Mr. Green patted him on the shoulder.

Walking toward the house, Steve thought, "He's just feeling sorry for me."

That evening, Steve tried to do his spelling, but somehow he could not keep his mind on it.

He looked up now and then to see if his mother was watching him. But he couldn't catch her eye.

For the next few days Steve tried to make up his mind about whether to go to the Open House.

One minute he thought how much fun it would be to surprise her with all the work he had on display. The next minute he thought how awful it would be to have everyone see him with his mother and no father.

"They'll think I'm just a mama's boy," he said to himself.

On Wednesday as Steve was leaving for school his mother asked, "Are we going tonight, Steve?"

Looking at her, Steve answered, "Yes."

He felt better. At least he had made up his mind. But he still had to face all his friends. That would be hard to do.

Steve stopped at the small neighborhood park that afternoon. An old man was sitting on a bench, feeding some pigeons. Steve sat down next to him.

It was fun watching the birds. The old man smiled from time to time.

Steve wasn't sure if the old man was smiling at him or the pigeons.

Time went by so quickly that Steve almost forgot to go home. The big church clock struck five. Steve waved to the old man and hurried away.

As he opened the door he felt a funny sort of excitement. He wanted to go to the Open House and at the same time he didn't.

"Hurry, Steve," Mrs. Blakeman said. "I've been waiting for you. Let's eat early and leave so that we can get good seats."

When Steve finished dressing, he took a wristwatch from his drawer and put it on. It was too big for his thin wrist. It had been his father's watch.

Steve pushed the wristwatch halfway up his arm and put on his jacket. It felt good to wear something that had belonged to his dad.

Steve and his mother got to school early, but they weren't the first ones there.

Lisa came with both of her parents. But Eric came with his mother. Steve wondered if Eric had a father. He had never thought about it before. But he wouldn't ask Eric now.

Steve looked for Billy to see if he really had two mothers and two fathers. But all he could see was the top of Billy's head in a crowded corner.

Parents and other visitors began looking at the children's work. Steve had a surprise for his mother. His science exhibit had won an award. His painting was hanging where everyone could see it.

Soon it was time to find seats for the program. Steve turned around to see how many people were sitting in the rows of chairs.

Suddenly someone waved at Steve.

"Look!" he whispered, touching his mother's arm.

There was Uncle John in his uniform. Grandpa was with him. He was all dressed up, too. They walked toward Steve and his mother. Behind them came Mr. Green, their neighbor.

Steve was still feeling surprised as he moved over to make room for the three men.

The program was beginning.

Now Steve had a good feeling. He smiled as he thought how things had worked out. No one could really tell whether he had a father or not.

He turned around to see if anyone was looking at him. But no one was.

"That's funny," thought Steve. "I guess that everyone is too busy to notice me—except for my own family and Mr. Green."

Steve put his hand on the big wristwatch to keep it from falling off. It had been his father's, and now it was Steve's.

All at once Steve remembered his father. Somehow thinking about him didn't seem to hurt quite as much now. Then everyone began to laugh at the Punch and Judy show put on by some of the second graders. Steve laughed, too.

That night when Steve got into bed, he was happy, really happy, for the first time in a long while. When his mother came in to tuck him in, he put his arms around her neck and gave her a big hug.

About the Author and the Artist

MURIEL STANEK is the principal of a Chicago public school, and if this suggests an impersonal relationship to children, the assumption is soon proved false. To an amazing degree, Miss Stanek knows the girls and boys in her school and the things that trouble them. Her books illustrate her concern for children and reflect her experience in inner-city schools: *New in the City* is about an Appalachian boy who is a newcomer to city living; *One, Two, Three for Fun* is a counting book with city playgrounds for a setting; *Left, Right, Left, Right* tells how hard it is to learn directions; and *Tall Tina* is the story of a child taller than anyone else in the class.

Muriel Stanek was born and grew up in Chicago. She received her professional training at the University of Chicago. Although she had always loved reading, she did not think about becoming a writer until after she had begun teaching. Her first book was published in 1964, and she has produced educational materials as well as fiction and picture books. For hobbies she enjoys learning about and collecting prints and antique paintings.

ELEANOR MILL lives and paints in Manhattan, but she spent her childhood traveling from coast to coast. Before she finished high school in Maryland she had attended more than twenty different schools. She studied at the Corcoran School of Art in Washington, D.C., and for a year sketched portraits in National Park there.

Drawing, dancing, singing, and reading fairy tales were Miss Mill's favorite occupations as a child, and Arthur Rackham's mystical illustrations have remained an inspiration. While she has illustrated for magazines, textbooks, and Department of Education publications, she finds picture books her most satisfying assignments. She created the title character for Janice May Udry's *What Mary Jo Shared*, and the little girl she drew has become a living child to many young readers.